Chronicles of a Swordsman:

The Handmaiden's Diary

by Ian Z Gray

ISBN: 9781088152775

ISBN: 9781088152843(ebook)

First Paperback Edition March 2021

For the dungeon divers of old, dragon slayers that are yet to be, and all who dream of telling the tale of their time spent as another person, in another world.

Acknowledgments

This story is much less a product of my imagination and more of a story told around a campfire. Replace the fire itself with dice and a grid and you'll have a better idea of the world that Liam Morgan created for us. There would be no handmaiden's diary without him. There would be no depth to the narrator without the rest of the party who helped form him, and there would be no companions without the rest of the table. Thanks Nick Reynoso, Ian Soltes, Dan Moss-Colodny and Ed Calderon.

Also, a special thanks to those who let me read this to them while I was still working on it.

Prologue

You hold an ancient diary. The smell of smoke lingers on its charred edges. Roughly half its contents are burned away, and the discolored pages barely cling to its spine. Oddly, the first legible page is ascribed atop the marks of fire, in a much more recent ink. It reads, in a rather grandiose style of calligraphy, 'The Diary of a Handmaiden,' and below that, 'A Historical Manuscript Concluded and Narrated by Maximilian Napoleon Luciano Donnadieu.'

Though the first entries are rather mundane, the original author had a common recurring sentiment. She was hoping for the fall of 'The Sylvan Domain'. Specifically, she was seeking an opportunity to personally aid in its destruction. According to the author, that kingdom was overbearing towards the people of the continent. It postured its military might to oppress many nations that peacefully coexisted otherwise.

The consistency breaks from the journal's more trivial contents with this entry:

> Finally, I've heard word! My excitement can't pour out of this pen fast enough! It's been made official. No more waiting, no more fact-checking (and re-re-re-checking). We have the strategy and agreement from all parties. We can cripple their army in one fell swoop! It will be a slow and calculated process to set up, sure, but it will be an active one. Best of all, I'll have the honor of being one of the

moving cogs myself. I'm to use my... 'wits'... and all other tools at my disposal to herd that group of beasts into our trap.

I'm equal parts excited and grateful. I'll see this through with the highest level of precision and detail. I'll gather my entire lifetime's worth of luck, and all the effort I can muster in my bones. Even when I sleep, I'll play an active part. Supplies arrive this afternoon. Until then, I'll have to devise a way to hide this journal (or 'little piece of history in the making' HA!) and prepare my 'mask'. Tomorrow I start my new job...

Entries are dated less frequently from that point forward:

Damn, it's been weeks and I've barely been in his presence more than five minutes. Who knew he'd be such a shut-in? He even goes so far as to take his meals alone in his study. I was told I'd be placed in a position that was closer to him. Right now, the one who brings him his bread and clears his plates spends more time alone with him than anyone else. One more week of patience, then I'll have to act on my own. I'm willing to die for our cause, but I am not willing to spend a lifetime as a handmaiden on a fruitless effort.

The entry that follows:

I was sad to hear that the food runner fell ill. Which is strange, since I'm the one who poisoned her. I took her hand in front of one of the cooks and promised to fill the role for her out of kinship while she took time to recover. 'Kinship,' had we even exchanged names? Well since she will likely never recover, that secures my spot at his side for now.

The man barely looks up from his work when he eats. It was by the second meal of the second day that I stopped between his door guards and his desk to unbutton my top and hike my bottoms. I only had to hesitate in leaving a second or two longer before I could hear it. 'What happened to the last one who would bring my meals?' I made sure to exaggerate my bending to pick up the fork I 'dropped' on my second way out.

The entries continue with:

He took my advice! It was small, but it needs to be at first. He wore his blue scarf instead of his green. I told him it brought out his eyes and tried to make myself blush as if it wasn't me who suggested he wear it the day before. Hahaha! He was more talkative today too. Asked more questions. Lucky I never stopped rehearsing my backstory in my head.

Eventually:

Apparently, his wife is as shrewd as she is beautiful. I caught a plain-faced scowl from her after I gave him one of my fake laughs. She must have heard me from the hall before she entered. A half a dozen other handmaidens in the parlor and she knew it was me. I'll have to be more careful. She might be clever but I'm patient. She might be pretty, but I'm younger. And I'm new.

Somewhere towards the end of the entries:

> I almost feel bad for the man. He *actually* thinks that he loves me. To his credit though, my life's significantly easier now than it's ever been. Better chambers, nicer clothes, a piece of jewellery here and there. A man who listens to me.
>
> When his wife's away his entire wing is my private, giant suit. Though she spends more time away than here, there are always annoying reminders that she'll return.
>
> Her image in their portraits. The closets full of gowns in the style reserved for those who were born with the right to wear them. The smell of her perfume on the pillow in my place in the bed beside him. ...and he does keep me close to his side...

Which is exactly what I wanted from the start.

Almost lastly:

Maybe I should just give it up. Appreciate this new life I fell into. Stop sneaking off to the contact points for secret messages. Stop sending out the intel. Let myself have a child? Live this pampered life above instead of a rebellious one below?

He really is a sweet man.

Betray everything I ever knew? For a life of calm?

The final entry from the original author reads:

It's underway. Tomorrow. I'll be close when it happens.

The page to the right of that entry is left blank. Turning the page again reveals that a bit more was recorded. Although, instead of half faded diary entries, the same much-more-recent looking ink as before fills the pages. With it, there are both lengthy bits of writing and sketches dotted with the occasional drip of color. Overall, on top of the remaining half-burnt time-stained pages, seems to be the telling of a story.

SECTION I

Prelude to the Final Act

It's said if you follow the right cave long enough, you'll discover a gateway to the realms beneath. Cut off and guarded by the dogs of hell are hidden truths and treasures beyond the reach of man. The border between mortals and those which induce death. If you've ever known fear, you've known the forces that dwell there.

What If I told you, there were even greater forces? Heroes so mighty they no longer need to endure the cruel laws of nature that once bound them. Those who can dive into depths so deadly they'd poison the very souls of lesser men. The story I tell here may be of the triumph of those heroes. It may also be of the realm that lies beyond the cave. A wise reader may ask, "Is this a tale of something else entirely? Something eternal, something carnal, something born when the line between purity and pain is not merely crossed but broken?" Perhaps...

Three mighty forces traverse a deepening cave. They carry on past rigid stalagmites and through course, uneven walls. As the reach of light wanes, the walls become smooth until a carved archway is in view. Beyond it is the vestibule. So nobly the light stretches just inside. Though, it's sadly reached its limit. A clear border is drawn between the known and unknown. A man steps one pace farther than the courage of the sun. His figure masked from view by the shadows sleeping in the realm below, he reaches for his tool of choice. He bears his own light.

~~~

A lantern, now placed on an aged crate reveals the markings and masonry of the vestibule. "Almost Dwarven," says his smooth, calm voice, "... Almost."

His companions need not aid from the lantern to view their surroundings. Their kind is born destined to stare into the abyss. Not all heroes are born with a destiny, however. Some birth their own. He squints his eyes to see the edge of an archway and lights a torch. The room's now all but identified for its true nature, a distraction. A harbinger of hesitation. A place to gather one's footing and take a final breath before diving into the sea of the deadly.

With an effortless toss, his torch lands through the archway. It illuminates a well-carved hall. Curiously, the light is changing. The once yellowish glow is green. Its flames are now turquoise. A chill permeates the bones of the three companion forces.

The sound of footsteps echoes through the glowing hall. They gain speed. They gain number. They draw closer. The true nature
~~~

of this archway is now clear to the man. It's both the exit from a place of peace and the entrance to a house of death. He smiles. Someone must have forgotten to tell death the type of man he is. He brings his own peace with him.

"The damned invaders are down this way," a voice shouts, "I heard them!"

"Show me!" yells another.

"Yes," shouts the hero, "Which way are the invaders?"

The footsteps stop. Halting to a mere phrase from his lips. The hold is brief, however. The confusion fades and the first foes enter view. Emitting a turquoise glow of their own are armoured Elven soldiers. Their color gives them an eerie translucence. Ghosts. Angry Ghosts.

With no prompt needed, the thrusting force charges into view through the light of the lantern. The largest kobold you'll have ever seen, with his sturdy lance, strikes the shield of the closest ghost. As the hum of his strike vibrates through his lance, he loses no ground. He's harnessing ferocity itself.

One more strike drives clear through the

ghost's torso until it vanishes completely. He moves and strikes again, crushing the will of a second ghost's armour. It too vanishes. The man stares in awe of the lancer. His name's Giantslayer, a kobold who can transfer vigour through his lance just as an artist would transfer beauty through their paintbrush.

Five more ghosts find their way around the corner. The force of magic acts. Her half-elf form illuminated by a ball of fire she summons in her hands. It shoots directly to the huddle of ghosts and expands rapidly. A bright red explosion engulfs all ghosts in view. The man shields his eyes. Flames shoot from the archway! The faint turquoise glimmer of the torch remains, but all the ghosts are gone. She takes an audible breath. She's Caelynn, an elf who aspires to be a queen.

The torch changes again. It glows brighter. More are coming! As quickly as they vanished from the hall, new ghosts refill it like a new wave fills a sandy shore. This time a soldier of considerable rank joins them. A general. It's time for the third force to act. Before the general can unsheathe his sword, the man is upon him. Swift and agile, with two swords at the ready, he does not draw.

Lit now from the turquoise glow of his torch, and the orange hue from his lantern behind him, he can finally be seen. Eternity trapped within a glance. The ghost general locks eyes with a man who's no stranger to being recorded in stories. It's the famed hero Maximilian Napoleon Luciano Donnadieu! Yes, *that* Maximilian Napoleon Luciano Donnadieu. He bows his head and kneels before the general.

But surely, you ask, if it's truly him then why doesn't he unsheathe his swords and lay waste to the ghostly warriors? Why not use his legendary skills, mobility, and agility to pierce their ghostly hearts and end this skirmish in a mere instant? Well, the answer is a simple one. While, yes, he *could* take swift action and cut down yet another general that stands before him or destroy yet another army, there's something you must learn about the third member of this party. He is the force of benevolence.

"I am the *famed* hero Maximilian Napoleon Luciano Donnadieu," He said in elvish as he bows, "ally to the helpless, friend to the forgotten, sword for the empty-handed, and protector of those who cannot protect themselves. I've served many times in aid to the Sylvan domain, preserved the lives of many of its citizens, and brought an end to many of its foes. A soldier of your great stature has surely heard of me." Behind the general scores of elven ghosts charge through the hall ready to engage in battle. The hero continues, "I've come to offer my swords and aid in slaying... whatever it is that you're struggling with right now."

The general eyes the party doubtfully. "We're here to fight the alliance between the dwarves and humans who've invaded our territory. I'm not sure what help you'll be, but if you truly wish to aid the sylvan domain then so be it." He turns and runs with the scores of charging troops. As the man stands, the party regroups. Caelynn brings his lantern. They find a way past their first obstacle and through the archway by running alongside the ghostly army...

To answer your question, *yes*. Maximilian Napoleon Luciano Donnadieu is not only known as a great hero, who's so widely beloved that his existence is sometimes even questioned by those who've met him, but also as a humble artist. Yes, some of his paintings hang among national treasures in historic galleries. Yes, his sketches can be found in priceless books and tombs across the realms. Yes, he *is* known to have authored great works such as "He who slew the greatest swordsman", "Blackbird Sings in the Dead of Night", and "A Dance of the Heart". Finally, yes you cunning reader, it's his name you read in the title as the author of this story.

It is I, Maximilian Napoleon Luciano Donnadieu who narrates this tale. This much I will reveal to you now. Who else could provide such a detailed, first-hand account of this tragic story's second half but one who's simultaneously so battle-tested and poetic as me? To be honest, now that you've put the pieces together, I'm not only proud of you, but I welcome this transition into the first-person narrative. But will I be alive to narrate the end? That is yet to be revealed.

So, as I stood with a ghostly torch in hand, the party regrouped. Caelynn brought me my lantern. We found a way past our first obstacle, entered through the archway, and ran alongside the ghostly army...

Maximilian Napoleon Luciano Donnadieu

CAELYNN

GIANTSLAYER

No Wall Too Small

Door after door flew by as we made chase with our former foes. We raced to the unknown, knowing only that danger awaited us. What could be so terrible that an endless army of ghosts would consider it a worthy threat? We hoped to find out sooner rather than later. This hallway seemed endless - '*Slam!*'

Down fell a spiked gate just in front of us. Yes, of course, *I* nimbly evaded certain death by stopping just in time, but my party members? As the ghosts continued their chase through the gate, I checked them. Both were unharmed but not unmoved. The gate missed Giantslayer's body but sliced through his patience.

"Giantslayer is tired of this endlessly *small* hallway and its *tiny* traps! No gate door is too sturdy to keep the *massive* Giantslayer contained!" He reached to the floor, grabbed the gate, and heaved. His form was magnificent! Lifting from his legs, not his back, demonstrated his experience. His tight grip and bulging eyes demonstrated his ferocity. His clenching, rock-hard glutes demonstrated his great thrusting force as his hips drove towards the gate and he rose from the ground. The gate rose with such power that it flew up from his hands. A '*click,*' was heard from what must have been a locking mechanism. In unison, we ran again.

~~~

We saw the hall's end; a large room cut into the stone with a row of shields at the back. Entering the room was curious. Where
~~~

had all the charging elves gone? There were only a few ghosts marching steadily into the room. I tossed my turquoise torch ahead. It revealed a row of dwarven ghosts who wielded massive shields. They lined the room from end to end. Behind them ghosts of human soldiers wielded pikes. The elves moved into formation. Giantslayer broke the silence again.

"Giantslayer questions the strategical advantage of your current defensive formation. This is a *small* strategy that Giantslayer will easily penetrate with his *massive* lance!" His glutes tightened. He was ready to thrust.

Giantslayer charged towards the right-hand wall. Lance clashed with shield! A brief echo. An unstoppable force met with an immovable object. He struck again, this time missing completely. His lance buzzed. The power of the dwarven defense must have taken him by surprise; the initial clash throwing off the aim of his successive strikes.

"Are you kidding me," Caelynn put one hand on her head and pointed the other towards the fighting, "I just want to fireball them, but everyone's too close together!" It was my time to act. The iron defense of these dwarves was so daunting, I knew my party needed to witness a successful strike to maintain their morale. For the sake of their hearts, I threw myself towards pointed pikes and a wall of ghosts. I heard one last 'clang' of Giantslayer's lance as I began my move.

As I dashed towards the left, the opposing soldiers braced at the ready. In the blink of an eye, I was but a pace and a half from a dwarven shield. Then I was free. Free from the shackles of the ground beneath my feet, I leaped into the air. My feet moved towards the ceiling as I reached for my trusted swords. The dwarf's eyes met mine as I mounted the peak of my somersault. With legs stretched skywards and swords fully drawn, I spun like a dreidel. I could feel the dwarf's awe at the sight of me while dazzling light danced off my swords, my espadas roperas, as I spun. The legendary pitch-black rapier Jezebel, with her emerald bejewelled guard. The famed and beloved Freya, pearl white from pommel to point.

I landed as a cat - softly and without noise. Jezebel struck first. She pierced through the back of the dwarf. His shield sank heavily from the pain. Freya searched for the heart of one of the pikemen. His translucent glow blurred the edges of his frame. The pikeman was missed. I stepped back out of reach of the dwarves and signalled to the party that all would be well. Their defenses would fall. They were clearly reassured.

The elves made their move. Swords clashed against shields, but no ground was gained. The pikemen struck through the shields of their allies. Two elves fell. I watched as a pike found its mark on Giantslayer's scaly hide. Distracted, I took a blow to my shoulder. The pikeman demanded my attention. A light blared quickly towards Giantslayer. It was Caelynn's magic. The blast of frost found its mark on a dwarf. I was reminded of my purpose behind this enemy's line.

I glanced at the pikeman, ignoring my instinct to riposte. Giantslayer's screams echoed among the sounds of metal against metal. I lunged back at the dwarf who'd already acquainted himself with Jezebel and reintroduced them. Then came Freya; piercing through the back of the ghost dwarf until there was nothing left of him at all. I shouted, "The wall is broken!"

The dwarfs made their move. Flanking the elves to box them in. Metal found metal and ghostly flesh. In seconds, soldiers from both sides fell. Caelynn sent more magic towards the right end of the wall. There were then two breaches in their fence of iron!

Giantslayer's large voice was heard among the clashing bells of war. "Having twice as many pikemen followed by a third row of archers or even stone-throwers would have been a much *bigger* strategy for this particular defensive situation you've found yourselves in!" Two dwarves vanished as he shouted about the finer points of situational battle formation.

The pikeman tested me again. This time I was at the ready. Breaking through my opponent's wall of shields took me but a hop. For him to breach the defenses of the shield-less hero he found before him proved much more difficult. For it's Jezebel and Freya who guard my flesh. His pike, like lightning, reached toward me. Freya disagreed. The pike found no mark but the air beside me. While the glimmering jewels on Jezebel's guard briefly distracted the pikeman's eyes, Freya seduced his heart with her razor point. He vanished only an instant before Jezebel broke yet another hole in their defense. A second Dwarf extinguished itself around one of my blades. The elves encircled the broken wall.

I turned toward the other side of the room. A noticeable frost covered the armour of several dwarven soldiers. Giantslayer was laying waste to both pike and shield. An elven lieutenant moved through the gap that Giantslayer and Caelynn carved and clashed with a pikeman. He was at once surrounded. I swiftly closed the distance between us, dancing through raindrops of ghostly pikes as I moved. My espada ropera vanished the men at his flanks. It was the first time, I saved someone whose life was already long lost. In place of a pike through his neck, he won a wink from a famed hero. A glimmer of hope. He regained his composure and continued to slash away at the remaining opponents.

What elves remained aided my companions and me in cutting down the final soldiers, regrouped, and marched through the corridor beyond. My party and I paused to examine what was out of place. There were skeletal remains, piles of dust, and rusted armour.

Giantslayer slammed the bottom of his fist into his other hand twice and shook his head. "I can't believe they didn't have a third row containing archers!"

Caelynn brushed off her clothes calmly. "Does anybody need to rest?"

"Giantslayer can press on, but these skeletons appear to be worth noting. It seems only the ghosts slain by other ghosts remained in their proper positions." He rubbed his hand over his long jaw as he thought. "Giantslayer can't speak for everyone's personal experiences, but it appears as though the ghosts that *we* eliminated did not leave rubble at their feet."

I continued surveying the room. "I can confirm that. What do you think is the likelihood these remains rise and flank us once we're deeper inside? ...Who thinks we should burn them?"

"Giantslayer is not a superstitious man, but even Giantslayer thinks it's a very *small* idea to mess with these ancient, cursed remains. Especially before we traverse deeper into this unknown landscape that appears to be stuffed full of *massive* necromantic power!"

The mage shrugged. "Ghosts don't usually leave remains when they're killed. The elves we killed before didn't leave anything behind, remember?"

"Giantslayers starting to believe there's some *sick*, endless cycle of pain encompassing the souls that fought in this place; and we will only find answers by making our way farther inside."

We did just that. I stopped tallying the number of archways and corridors we passed through after growing bored of counting. Our lancer described, in detail, half a dozen different formations the ghosts could've used which he determined would've been more effective than what they met us with. Caelynn teased him; asking rudimentary questions and follow-ups that required exhaustive explanation. He was too wrapped up in the lecture to notice the sarcastic tone she liked to take when she wasn't being earnest.

There were no ghosts by our sides as we ventured further into the unknown. Eventually, there were no walls by our sides either. We entered a great opening at the edge of what appeared to be a cliff. I dropped my turquoise torch. It plummeted, revealing the edges of a descending spiral walkway about forty levels deep.

As the light found its bottom, the sounds of battle echoed back up. Torches adorning the spiral lit from the bottom of the pit. Like a corkscrew, turquoise light spiralled along the walkway. It revealed the clash of ghostly soldiers as the sounds of lighting flames ushered in the crashing noises of war. Metal upon metal, screams of pain, orders being yelled, all could be heard through the entire depth of the spiral.

I looked my party over. Our lancer seemed sapped of his vigour. Our mage appeared dizzied. While my skills are not the kind that are hindered by daily limits, it's that very perseverance that allows me to maintain my concern for the well-being of my beloved party. "Well, I suppose if we're to get any rest, we should do it now."

Caelynn raised her hand. "I second that." She let her traveller's pack drop to the ground with a relieved sigh and sat on it.

The kobold pointed to the ceiling and quickly paced in a zigzagging line. "Giantslayer's knowledge of infrastructure causes him great concern for the innocent people living in the city above. This is a sinkhole! We need to clear the ghosts out of here so the city council can have workers install support beams. We have to warn them of this impending threat," he paused and looked back at us, "Also Giantslayer would like to rest here too!"

As we set up camp, we were met with another ghostly figure. This one, unlike the soldiers we'd seen before, wore no armour and wielded no weapons. His clothes appeared far eastern in fashion. "And who might you be?"

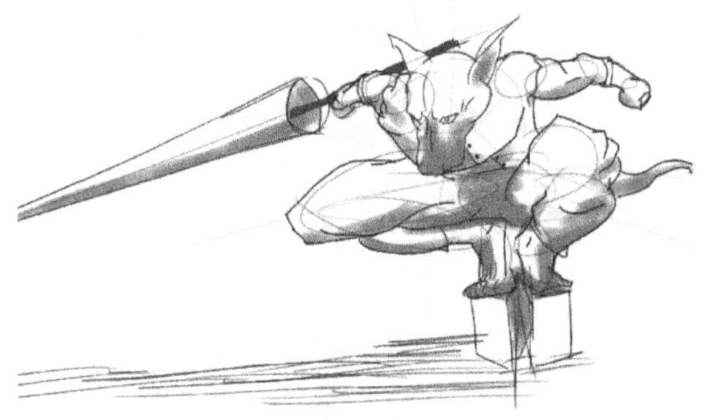

GIANTSLAYER

CAELYNN

While Caelynn and Giantslayer bickered over camp preparations, it seemed I had a private audience with this mysterious new guest. His hand placed on his chin, he darted his eyes between the hall we entered from and my party. I stepped closer to him and asked again, "Excuse me. Who, might I ask... do I *presently* have the pleasure of making acquaintance?"

"This certainly is very interesting," he

dropped his hands to his side as he moved toward me, "I'm Ardronel. I've been stuck inside this city for ages and have seen many adventurers attempt to enter. All, of course, lost their lives or eventually retreated, but none have been able to do what you did..."

"Well, it's to be expected. A group of this calibre is rare to come by. You are, after all, in the presence of Maxim-"

"Maximilian, yes. Donnadieu was it?"

I smiled.

"I was listening earlier. As I said I've been here for... at least a few thousand years I would imagine. Now for a time, I was," He motioned around us, "just as the others still are. Trapped in an endless cycle. Day after day, I relived my last hours alive until eventually re-experiencing my death." He put his hand on his chin, "Somehow... I managed to become aware of what was happening to us all. Though I eventually detached from the repetition, my soul is not yet free."

I tried to console him. "That sounds terrible."

"Um, who's this?"

"Ah, Caelynn. This man was just informing me that our names are even known beyond the reach of mortal ears."

"Giantslayer demands that you identify yourself!"

He held out his hands in defense. "Oh, I assure you both that I'm no threat. I was just speaking with your friend here-"

"Yes, he told me that while other adventurers have failed to make it as far as us, some of them must have discussed our tales so loudly that he could hear."

"Well, no, I said I heard you speaking earlier."

"He even heard us speaking," I reiterated.

"Giantslayer doesn't like asking the same question multiple times!"

"Giantslayer," I tapped his back and gestured toward Ardronel, "he's a fan."

"Well, this may be, but none of that changes the fact that we've been battling ghosts since arriving here, and he is most certainly another ghost."

"Oh, that might be a sensitive subject," I whispered.

"No need to worry. I've long since made peace with my fate."

"Even so, I'm sorry for your loss."

The spirit paused with an almost confused expression. "Thank you." He turned to Giantslayer with his hand on his chest, "I'm Ardronel. I was one of the diplomats here from a nation not engaged in this battle."

Caelynn shrugged with one hand, "So what happened?"

He gazed at the ceiling. "This city was once not only the home of a great nation but also an alliance between several races and kingdoms. While you've only encountered soldiers, there were also representatives from other nations here. It was serving as a meeting ground between us for a time."

"I'm not exactly sure why, but," He looked us in the eyes, "one day the elves attacked. They sought to slaughter everyone inside, regardless of nation, military affiliation, or rank. I was one of those slain. The battle raged as the countless elves eventually made their way down to the great hall. The place of the final skirmish."

The mage frowned. "Who won?"

"Well, isn't it obvious-"

"Tell them the part about how no one was able to do what we were!"

"Ah. Well since the invasion, the souls trapped here continually re-experience the day of their death. I'm not sure how yet, but through your actions, you were able to change the events slightly. Until now, besides my awakening, of course, nothing changed at all." Ardronel gazed again at the ceiling of the spire above us.

I gave a proud glance to my companions for their deeds before reaching into my satchel. I retrieved parchment and pen and made my mark on the page. Caelynn crossed her arms impatiently. "What exactly changed?"

"Well, the deaths and that skirmishes outcome... was overall slightly different..."

I joined in his gaze. "What are you staring at?"

"Oh, the sun moving into the horizon... it's my time to go soon."

I squinted at him. "The sun?"

Giantslayer shook his head and stepped

away. "There's officially no longer any credibility to this ghost's statements."

"Ardronel, I don't see *anything*. We're in a cave."

"There's a city above us," Giantslayer shouted!

His eyes darted to the kobold. "A city? No, this whole area has always been an open space. ...So, there's a ceiling now." He brought his hand to his chin and shifted his posture.

Caelynn's expression fell flat, and she looked at me. "Okay, how is that not something you notice when you're here for, like, ever?"

"Maybe the curse is forcing us to see what once was."

"Well, it couldn't have happened overnight."

"It's always been the same open space to me. Every day was the same... except once when the sky fell..."

She dropped her arms and tilted her head at him like a dog. "The sky fell?"

"This adds to Giantslayer's growing concern of the structural support problems here."

"I have to go. Since you changed things here then maybe if you make it deeper in the city; to the final fight, you can change even more."

"Well then," I finally handed him the signed parchment, "as I'm sure you've been waiting to ask for, here is my autograph."

Ardronel was shocked. For a hero, he heard tales of to not only converse with him in person but to offer a personal token of himself clearly stunned him. It was likely the most exciting event to transpire for him in *thousands* of years. He retrieved the autograph from my hand. Unfortunately, his ghostly form soon got the better of him. After only a moment, it phased from his grasp as he slowly sunk into the ground below him. "I must go now." He fell out of view.

Caelynn rolled her eyes. "Well, that told us nothing."

I grabbed my lantern. "Nothing but to press on as planned."

~~~

With my companions well-rested, we
~~~

proceeded down the spiralling city. Ghostly torches adorning the walls lit our view as we approached them. The open edged walkway grew a wall as we descended. Sounds of battle rang from adjacent halls as we passed. The occasional straggling soldier was dispersed with relative ease. These distractions did nothing to delay us. Our path was clear.

We were eventually presented with a more persistent distraction. Through a hall just ahead walked a massive person. He stood at least eight feet tall, wore well-kept plated armour, and held a greatsword on his back. His skin bleached white with thick contrasting lines throughout his face. Interestingly, he was no ghost. "Oh," he said, "you all."

I smiled. "It certainly is."

Giantslayer marched up to him. "I would like to know who you are and how you got here."

"Yeah, how *did* you get here?" Caelynn added.

"Well, I got here following probably the same information as you and sneaked right past you while you rested." He surveyed our surroundings inquisitively. "My name's Beatstick. I'm a mercenary, like you."

"Thank you for sharing so quickly." The kobold's posture relaxed, and he pointed his fingers to identify us. "Giantslayer, Maximilian, Caelynn. Although Giantslayer feels the need to inform you that we are not mercenaries."

Caelynn approached the man and outreached her hand to him. "Well, you must be pretty strong to make it past these dangers alone. How about we all go the rest of the way together?"

He ignored her hand and turned away from it. "Dangers? The most dangerous thing I've seen so far is you lot napping by the edge of the cliff at the top of this pit. How are you not mercenaries by the way?"

"Well, Giantslayer was once a soldier, but my current role is to investigate the depths here for the sake of the people above."

Beatstick smirked. "Did you get hired by someone to investigate this?"

"You could say that. Giantslayer did ask

for compensation in exchange for the services requested of him."

"Then you're a mercenary."

I smiled and held up my hand. "Well, the title I'm usually referred to as is 'hero of the people', but you may call me what you wish if you will truly aid in my current quest. Shall we continue down?"

"I don't see why not."

The kobold huffed as we walked. "Hold on-"

"So did you find anything important while exploring these rooms?" Caelynn motioned around the corridor.

"No, nothing important."

"Hold on, Giantslayer was a soldier and is definitely not a mercenary. Giantslayer can't stress this enough."

Beatstick squinted and raised an eyebrow at him. "So, why'd you come down here then?"

"As Giantslayer's sure you know, many adventurers have gone missing after entering the caves that brought us here. This underground area, that we now know is a giant sinkhole by the way and a *danger* to those above us, is clearly the cause."

"And the person who sent you here is paying you?"

"Well yes, but while Giantslayer believes and engages in fair trade, that does not make him a mercenary."

"Yes, it does."

I shrugged. "Well, I'm guessing this might be a while. I'm going to continue my way down if any of you would like to join me."

Caelynn raised a finger before moving past the arguing strongmen. "Yes please." We proceeded. The voices above us raised in volume as we moved further away, leaving us continually aware of the entire conversation.

"Look, Giantslayer's not judging you for your choices or identity. While a captain, he worked with and lead soldiers and mercenaries alike. Giantslayer just asks that you understand that he is no mercenary."

"Yeah, okay. But you're definitely mercenaries."

"Giantslayer was a soldier!"

"And now you're a mercenary."

"Giantslayer thinks you have a fundamental misunderstanding of what a mercenary is!"

...Eventually, both our new and old companion caught up as we continued our spiralling descent.

Beatstick

M AXIMILIAN
N APOLEON
L UCIANO
D ONNADIEU

SECTION II

Shifting Pieces on the Board

The spiral hallway gave way to a large open space. We slowed, anticipating an encounter. A shout called from the waiting darkness. Its words were meaningless to me. "Does anyone speak dwarvish?" My party looked among each other and grimaced.

The voice tried again, but in a language that we knew, "Come no further, invaders! This is the end of your journey," as he spoke, the familiar hue of torches flooded the room with light. Straight ahead, the ghosts of dwarven shield-men appeared in their rowed formation; three times longer than before. With them were not only the pikemen but a third row of soldiers. At their backs was a massive portcullis. Also wielding pikes, they guarded a central crowned figure, the king of the dwarves. "This has been our home for generations untold. Surrender or meet your death!"

We shouted our noble intentions, but our explanations fell on deaf ears. From our backs, a familiar voice made its own command, "All lands here have belonged to the sylvan domain since their creation. You are the invaders. Your generations of unauthorized occupancy do not excuse your crimes; past or current." The ghosts of the elven general and his troops surrounded us.

Beatstick turned to the elven soldiers and took an aggressive posture. "I won't let you attack these soldiers! If you want to kill them, then you'll have to go through me first!"

Caelynn threw up her arms looking at the kobold and me, "What? We never agreed to that!"

The dwarven king shouted, "I'm commanding you to leave my lands now!"

The general drew his longsword and pointed it at the king, "You have our permission to surrender now, but I assure you there's no need. All before us will die here today!"

Caelynn waved at the general and motioned towards us. "Wait, you don't mean us too, do you? Remember us, the group that was helping you this whole time?" She was ignored, as elves knocked their arrows.

"Mercenary," Giantslayer said, "We have been doing battle with the dwarven stronghold to make our way here. You risk doubling our current enemies." Beatstick faced the elven General and drew his sword. His presence was ignored. The general stared through him directly toward his goal.

Caelynn took a long step away from Beatstick and pointed at him. "Okay, we are *not* with him!" Both parties escalated their threats while my group gathered to quickly whisper a plan. "Okay," she said, "changing sides is one thing, but doing so while we're surrounded is not the time."

"The dwarves will likely attack us regardless at this point," I said.

"I'm not changing sides," Beatstick shouted, "I'm only striking the elves if they try to engage."

Giantslayer grabbed his shoulder. "This is an endless loop. We already know they'll engage. If you're so set on fighting the elves then fine, but first things first we need to take out the dwarves so we're not outnumbered on both sides."

"I said I'm fighting the elves!" He brushed away the kobold's hand.

"Then you're a fool."

The elven archers took aim. Caelynn's eyes darted around them. "Wait, you're not going to try to kill us, right?" They ignored her. Their focus was still eerily on the dwarven defense. The trance that compelled the ghosts into combat didn't allow them to sense us. We were invisible to them in both sight and sound. The dwarven shields readied. "Okay then, if we somehow could beat them both, that would end the curse, right?"

I wasn't so sure. Until that point, we did what was needed to progress. Though our goal was to cleanse the place, not conquer it. "Perhaps we should wait and see how this clash originally ended. That might reveal our answer."

"Giantslayer has never slain a king; living or otherwise. Ignoring rare opportunities like this will lead to a very *small* life." He drew his lance.

The dwarf king shouted, "It's you who'll meet his end here today!" Arrows loosed, and elves charged. I made my move! Sprinting towards the dwarves, I leaped again over their defenses. Once my feet met the ground, I unleashed my espadas roperas, seeking to create a sizable breach in the dwarven wall. While I laid a ghost to nothingness, I saw my companions.

Beatstick remained still, as Caelynn searched for cover. The attacking soldiers charged the defensive lines. Elven blades crashed against dwarven shields. Giantslayer sprinted toward the dwarves.

I anticipated the crash of his force against a sturdy shield, but the tip of his lance dropped downward. It struck the floor at a space between tiles. His hands gripped it tightly. With a mighty jump and the support of his lance below him, he vaulted over the dwarven lines! His overflowing vigour welled up inside me while I watched, with great pride, as the kobold showed his battle prowess by easily adopting my strategy. As his feet met the ground, a dwarf screamed and vanished.

I continued my assault. Like a fleeting kiss, the resistant force of dwarven armour gave way to the freedom of open-air as each soldier vanished on the tips of my blades. With no bodies left behind to hinder our movements, Jezebel and Freya lead me in a waltz to the sounds of crashing steel. Avoiding the thirsty points of ghostly blades, I caught glimpses of my companions as we spun.

Beatstick remained fixed in place; slashing any elves who tried moving past him. Several lost their footing from his maneuvers and toppled to the ground. They vanished as mighty slams from his sword broke through them and cracked the stone below.

Giantslayer closed the distance between us. His eyes bloodshot, his breathing heavy, he thrust again and again through the translucent armour of the dwarves while his gaze remained affixed to the dwarven king. Caelynn traversed the deadly battlefield, bolting frozen blasts at the dwarves while frantically avoiding the reach of elven warriors.

Beatstick held his form, bringing charging elves to the ground like apples from a shaking tree. Giantslayer dispatched the last of the king's guards, earning the attention of the noble. Dwarven sword met lance with mighty force! I heard Caelynn shout. "I can't fireball while I'm still surrounded." Her words maintained our fluid dynamic even while engulfed by the thirsty fangs of death. "I'll be clear in a couple seconds. Just tell me where to place it!" The general's attention on the dwarves finally broke. He strutted up to Beatstick. "Hold!" I replied to Caelynn.

The dwarf king continued clashing with Giantslayer's lance. The kobold lost no fervour, footing, or fury, and maintained his dominating thrusts at the ghostly ruler. Jezebel and Freya danced with frantic pikes. Beatstick came to blows with the general, neither yielding to each other's will. The mage freed herself from the reach of the elves, and finally - *AN EXPLOSION!*

On the edge of the battle, the wall close to Caelynn burst open! It wasn't from her magic. A flood of dwarves poured through the opening, slicing down elves in their path. "Guys, there's more of them! Ugh! I'm surrounded again! Should I fireball anyway? There's a lot of them!"

"Hold!" I judged the distance between us, searching for a route to her side! Freya erased the last ghost between myself and the king, though a path to my isolated companion was not yet clear. What I could see though, was our lancer, very clearly in view and not at all obstructed by the translucent form of the monarch. His opponent was slain. Rage still filled his eyes as he turned from me and continued his assault on the surrounding dwarves.

Beatstick stood over the elven general

who slashed away any attempts to finish him. Caelynn was but a few paces from being washed over by the wave of incoming ghosts. A breach carved out by our lancer revealed a path I could take to her. With all my speed, I could make it but a leap or two from her. I'd be in the centre of the reinforcements and could perhaps draw their attention, but could I survive the fiery explosion I'd soon ask her to place where I'd stand? I intended to find out!

Strangely, things weren't that simple. The ghosts began flickering. Their forms disappearing and reappearing like a moonlit glow on the ripples of a lake. Some froze in place. Some vanished and reappeared in a different spot. The general was again where he stood before the battle began. Other elves reset their positions as well, but the dwarven reinforcements remained.

Fortunately, so too, remained both the breach Giantslayer created, and the hole burst in the wall. Caelynn made use of the pause to find a safer position at the edge of the battlefield. *"All lands here have belonged to the sylvan domain since their creation."* It was time to make my move!

I returned my espadas roperas to their sheaths and drew my lantern. Quickly, I made my way through Giantslayer's gateway. *"I'm commanding you to leave my lands now,"* I heard behind me. I carved my way around the frozen dwarves and landed at my new destination, the edge of the blown wall. *"You have our permission to surrender now, but I assure you there's no need. All before us will die here today!"*

Faced with the confusion of the reformed battlefield, and the vast distance between us all, Caelynn pleaded again for guidance, "What do I do?" I pointed my lantern toward the abyss and looked solemnly back at her.

"Hold." I breached the horizontal abyss alone.

Beatstick

Caelynn

Alone into the Unknown

Guided by my lantern, I made my way through a hand-crafted hallway. I knew not what I'd find, but believed my answer waited ahead, if I could only find it. My beloved companions' dire need for my aide pained me, but I couldn't guess how often the ghosts would revive and surround us. At the top of the spiral, I already witnessed the limits of my party's stamina. To truly help them, I needed a way to cease the reanimation before exhaustion could overtake my group again.

Yes, reader, while separating from one's team is not typically the ideal battle scenario, famed heroes are never helpless. Being an expert duellist, and a fencer, I knew this narrow hallway would give me the advantage over any foe that found their way to me. A dwarf? A dozen? If the entire army waited ahead, it mattered not. They'd each have to take turns contesting this tireless hero if they'd hope to make it to the battlefield. Yes, these ghosts had been shown to appear out of nowhere and I could end up surrounded with no means of retreat. That risk, though, was the burden I chose to bear alone for the sake of my party's safety.

The hallway opened to a wide room. I found metals so rusted and worn that they were barely recognizable. These weapons, shields, and armour all lost the battle to time and turned to dust. While I traversed the defeated armoury, I imagined the souls trapped within these depths suffering similar decay. "How excruciating must their existence be?"

The room gave way to another

passage. Would this lead me to the end? The cure for the endless reanimation? Would I need to destroy a relic? Encounter more lingering spirits? Sure enough, a ghost did appear before me. It was Ardronel. He moved through the wall at my side. "You've done well to make it this far." His ethereal body blocked my path.

"Ah, Ardronel. Good to see you again."

"I feel the same. There's hope yet. While the ongoing struggle behind you was the climax of the invasion, I believe *your* final battle waits just ahead. I came to give you whatever support I can before that moment."

"You'll join us?"

He closed his eyes and shook his head. "I can't."

"Information then?"

"As much as I have."

"What should I be looking for? What will end all this?"

"I've searched these halls countless times but I'm still not sure what to look for. I've not found a single clue beyond this point." His expression became focused and serious.

"Know this: Once the battle behind you concludes, there will be a brief pause before the cycle starts again. If you can find a way to stop it here and now, there'll be no more cycles. It will finally end, and we can be free."

"Then what *will* I find ahead?"

"This path leads to the depths beyond the giant portcullis. At the bottom is the lowest hall in this city. While I've never found a solution, I strongly sense that you'll find it there." He walked out of sight through the wall, "I'll leave you to move ahead. Quickly, before it all starts again."

I took a step forward and paused. A vision of my companions flashed in my mind's eye. I knew I needed to continue forward and lift this curse before they became overpowered, but what if I wasn't swift enough? What if I returned to find their bodies strewn among ancient bones? I shuddered at the thought, and for fear of my companions' safety, rushed back to them!

Bursting through the blown wall, I discovered the accuracy of my instincts. The sight of the battlefield led the blade of dread straight through my heart. Ghost soldiers, nearly tipple in number, had outflanked my party on all sides. Caelynn was bracing herself inside a spherical shield of magic. Giantslayer, with his back pinned to the portcullis, was foaming at the mouth. Though there was no sign of the dwarven king, his guards slashed and stabbed at Giantslayer without relent. Beatstick stood still in the centre of the room, facing a figure I hadn't seen before.

An elven woman dressed in a tastefully designed white wizard's robe. The general was at her side. She stood still with her eyes locked on Beatstick. Her expression was puzzling; a mixture made from equal parts satisfaction and hatred. He spoke to her, though I couldn't hear his words. Behind her, I saw a chance to change our fates.

A momentary sliver of hope was carved in the dense conflict, a direct path between our mage and the elven wizard's back. I made my presence known with a thunderous call to action, "Caelynn! Fireball!" The words she'd waited to hear! She glanced at the white wizard, readied her spell, and – gone! Her target vanished. The room was empty.

The Portcullis

MAXIMILIAN
NAPOLEON
LUCIANO
DONNADIEU

SECTION III

The Divers of the Abyss

The party regrouped. "Giantslayer thinks we should make our way through that portcullis."

"Yes," I said, "though I've found that we can cross through the breached wall."

Caelynn was circling and inspecting each of us like a bird pecking for worms "Does anyone need healing? If we're going to rest at all, now's the time."

Beatstick shouldered his gear and started walking. "I don't think there's time for that."

"Giantslayer agrees." He popped a cork out of a vile and took a large gulp from a potion, "also, the centre of a necromantic cataclysm is a *small* place to loiter." He finished his potion as he walked. We moved through the armoury and its halls.

Caelynn hurried behind Beatstick. "Were you talking to that woman?"

"Yes."

"Did she say anything important?"

He paused between steps. "No."

"Giantslayer believes she's the cause of all this."

I rubbed my chin. "But how? She looked so young."

"Magic," Beatstick shrugged.

"That's a spell I'd like to learn," Caelynn chuckled.

"Or spells with an 'S'," he replied, "Either way, we'll find out soon. She said she's waiting ahead to kill us."

Caelynn threw her arms up at him and shouted, "That's important!"

~~~
~~~

We found our way through the passage. At our left was the giant portcullis. Giantslayer discovered the mechanism for opening that gate was destroyed. Its lever was melted. Opposite the gate, just as Ardronel said, was another spiralling descent. Though its walls were adorned with torches, they didn't ignite. I made use of them. With my espadas roperas at my sides, I was guided ever downward by a light in each hand.

"One of you has the key," said a voice I hadn't heard before. I couldn't place its location. It was as if my thoughts spoke to me.

Calynn's words were cautious. "Did anyone else hear that?"

"Giantslayer did."

I glanced at my companions. "I'm just now realizing that I've never asked this before, but... are any of you a ventriloquist?"

"I'm just glad this dungeon hasn't made me crazy," Caelynn sighed.

Beatstick shook his head. "No, it was definitely magic."

"Then is the better question 'did we all

hear the same thing?'"

"No," Beatstick said, "well probably not."

"A voice told me that one of us has the key," said Caelynn.

"Giantslayer heard that too."

"What did you hear, Beatstick?" I asked.

"That I have the key."

The spiralling path met its end. We arrived at the bottom in another large, empty room. The kobold spoke through clenched teeth. "Giantslayer would like to know what this *key* is, Beatstick."

Our new companion reached into his bag and retrieved a leather-bound notebook. "I found this in the room I was in before we met."

"Information we could have probably used before," the kobold grumbled.

Caelynn tilted her head and pointed her hand at him. "How is that not finding anything?"

"How is that a key," I asked?

"Look, it's a journal written by a spy that was posing as a handmaiden for the elven general. See for yourself."

As he described the entries within, I perused the pages. Its contents gave hints of subterfuge, murder, and lust. The skeleton of a contrived plot that led to terrible, unforeseen consequences. The diary held no end to the story within it. I knew it was one I must finish myself. Yes, dear reader, this is the very journal you hold in your hands! I placed it within my bag.

Caelynn crossed her arms and leaned into her hip. "So how does a handmaiden becoming a general's mistress create thousands of years of living purgatory?"

"That's the thing. I've studied plenty of ancient arcane legends. That's what..." He rubbed the back of his neck with one hand and squinted at us. "That's what *truly* lead me here... A prominent figure that went missing around the time of this kingdom's collapse was a white mage named Gwenovyn. I believe the white mage Gwenovyn was the elven general's wife."

"Giantslayer thinks we should pay more attention to the massive hole bore into the wall and floor here," he pointed beyond the reach of my eyes. I moved closer and saw it.

A massive tunnel burrowed through the stone room gaped in front of us. It was at least two men tall and four men wide. Its edges were eerily smooth, and it sloped downward.

"Have you found anything," asked a voice behind us.

"Ah, Ardronel," I said as we turned to him, "we found only a secret filled diary."

"Ghost... friend," asked Beatstick?

Caelynn waved her hands between them, "Oh yeah. Beatstick, this is Ar..don..el? We met him up at the top."

"Hello. Does the diary tell you where to go?"

"Well, no," I said, "but it seems like we'll continue through here."

"Through where?"

"The gaping hole," Beatstick snorted.

"The what?" We collectively threw our arms up and pointed at the massive hole directly behind us. "What are you all pointing at?"

Caelynn's expression fell flat. "You're kidding me."

"Giantslayer again questions the

reliability of our ghostly witness! First the ceiling and now this!"

Beatstick rose both eyebrows high and then crumpled them to squint. "Can you really not see this? It's a massive burrow through the stone."

He blinked. "I only see the stone wall that's always been here."

I sighed and motioned to the hole again. "It's no more a wall than the breach in the halls above us, dear friend."

Giantslayer stretched his back in a long, twisting motion. "Well, our destination is on the other side of your so-called wall, and we cannot afford any other delays."

"Agreed," said Beatstick.

I waited in place. "Will you finally join us?"

He gasped. "Th-through the wall? I don't think I can."

Caelynn shrugged. "Only one way to find out."

Ardronel fidgeted in place, "I... I've never ventured beyond this point... thousands of years-"

"Look, we've placed a *big* amount of

trust in you since we met. Giantslayer thinks it's time you placed a *proportionate* amount of trust in us."

With our eyes affixed to him, the ghost stepped closer. He breathed deep, closed his eyes, and, with us at his side, dove into the abyss. Step by step, his translucent blue form paled as he walked until he was completely white. He marched with us, our final companion in our descent.

"How much *longer* do you all plan on making me wait," the unknown voice shouted!

Beatstick

GIANTSLAYER

Sweet Maximilian, Lover of Love

We made haste through the narrow burrow until its walls expanded around us. I hurled my torches through dark unknown. A tiled floor was revealed around them, but the abyss's influence on my site persevered. The voice called again to the recesses of my mind. "Now, let's end this!"

Torches crackled as a yellow light glowed beside us. The ignition cascaded from torch to torch down the length of the room revealing all. We found the architect of the borrow. A mass of rocks and earth brought to life in a shape resembling a starved Ogre. Three paces behind it on either side were two well-dressed ghost warriors.

They wore crowns. One, the same dwarven king Giantslayer laid waste to some times before. The other, human. Against the wall on the far side of the room was the vessel of the voice. Centuries of heart-piercing agony personified: the floating ghostly form of Gwenovyn.

The earthly beast bellowed a cry of war as the torches changed to that familiar blue glow. The color cascaded again, this time, from the wall at Gwenovyn's back. The large, intricately carved, stone room was cast completely in its cool hue. With my eyes aided by the fires of her despair, I made no further delay.

Sprinting towards the enemy I drew my ebony blade and a special tool from my belt, a vile of acid. Before the hulking elemental made a move, I threw the vial at him. 'Crash!' It found its mark. The creature groaned and wiped its dripping eyes. I called Freya to my empty hand and stared down the human king.

Sweltering heat raced by me. The familiar sound of an explosion echoed among screams. My heart sank like a brick in a lake. Gwenovyn made her move, scorching my entire party with a massive ball of fire. Curse my leopard-like reflexes! Had I held form in defense of my beloved companions perhaps I could've swiftly taken the brunt of the attack myself? How easily she gained the upper hand by striking me where I bleed the most - my compassion.

I turned and saw a glimmer of hope. Our force of magic had her contingencies. Some of the flames blew towards Caelynn as if being pulled inside her very aura. She glowed red before placing her hand on Giantslayer's shoulder. His eyes widened, and he smiled through his teeth. The party was covered in soot but appeared to be alive an – Argh! Searing pain from my hip to shoulder!

The ghost had no need for pause. He made use of an opening in his opponent's defense with his fine crafted greatsword.

Our eyes met again while he squeezed his sword's grip in both hands; ready to cleave the weapon through me.

Here, the soul of an ancient king of man met a challenger he instinctively deemed worthy of his personal effort. The ageless soul of a king vs the body of a renowned legend still reaching his prime. His greatsword chopped down with the mighty force of gravity behind it.

Such a strike would need the aid of more finesse if it were to land a scratch on a swordsman like myself. With the same nimble reflexes that left my party behind me, I sidestepped the telegraphed arc of his strike. It crashed into the ground, creating a canyon in the finely carved stone floor. He swung again, spinning like a tornado. He struck me but caused no harm. My long-toothed bodyguards held him at bay like a barrier against my chest.

I heard the sprinting footsteps of my comrades, as the king and I clashed swords. "This *small* amalgamation of rocks will crumble beneath the boots of the *massive* Giantslayer!" The sound of a shovel digging deeply into earth preceded a visceral grunt from the elemental. Like a pickaxe burrowing through a mine of diamonds, I heard our lancer's strikes collide.

Jezebel pressed herself tightly against the king's greatsword; holding it still while Freya met his ghostly flesh. They danced with the mighty blade. It pushed through Jezebel's fleeting embrace and met only wind beyond her. I leaped back and to my party's line, ready to aid however they needed. Leaning behind a banister to survey the skirmish, I watched my gallant companions endure the onslaught.

Ardronel struggled against the dwarven king who was covered in a thick frost and making futile strikes at him. The king took blows from giant corporeal fists that mimicked the movements of Ardronel's arms while the white ghost steadily retreated from his reach. Pressed behind another banister at the far side of the room, Caelynn summoned flames between her hands.

She breathed deeply, willing the flames into a sphere. As it fired, it shrunk in size. Four bursts erupted from the mage's grasp.

Two struck the stone monstrosity's skull, and two reached Gwenovyn. She laughed as they were snuffed by a magical barrier.

Beatstick and Giantslayer were challenging the elemental. As the beast struck, the mercenary countered. He carved its hide while Giantslayer tried to penetrate it. The King of men was in pursuit. Joining the skirmish beside me, he swung at Beatstick. The first strike crashed against his sturdy shield. Like a cyclone he swung again, breaching the towering mercenaries' defenses.

Giantslayer roared again, thrusting deeply inside the elemental's gut. It groaned as he continued his onslaught, evading its metal hammer fists with ferocity fuelling his attacks. He used the creature's outstretched arm as a ramp and sprinted to its shoulders.

Recovering his lance to its full draw, he attacked the beast for the third time within my view. I gazed on as Giantslayer, with what must have been the absolute tightest that his stone sculpted glutes could have squeezed, so deeply thrust his mighty lance that it crashed straight through the elemental's skull! It shattered like glass. The beast bellowed no more as it collapsed into a pile of dirt on the ground.

The lancer was not satisfied. He stomped over his conquest's corpse and raced straight to Gwenovyn for one final mighty blow. She smiled as he approached. Halfway through his lunging strike another barricade formed around her. A wall of shields affixed to dwarven ghosts encircled her, intercepting his attack. Giantslayer's lance vibrated violently as it buzzed from the crash.

Beatstick swung twice at the king. While his blows did not land directly, he managed to loosen the ghost's footing and create the ideal space for me to make my move. I returned to view within the battlefield, espadas roperas in my hands. While bolts of magic and Ardronel's corporeal fists vanished the dwarven king, I moved into a duellist's position against my foe. The eyes of the ancient king of men met once more with my own. They were the last sight he'd view upon this world. Jezebel released him.

I made no pause for sentiment. Turning towards Gwenovyn, I ran to Giantslayer's side. My instincts rang out to me! Rather than continue to sprint beside him, I held up my swords in defense. My intuition proved true. Like a spark igniting a torch, several more elf soldiers appeared wielding swords! Two surrounded Ardronel, cutting through his guard. Two more surrounded Giantslayer. They cleaved through his scales as he screamed! One appeared beside me. My famed blades, at the ready, defended me from his strike. Blast! Behind me, another ghost slashed through my back.

I caught a glimpse of Caelynn emerging from the banister. She shot icy blasts in Ardronel's aid. They found their marks with ease. Beatstick chased beside me. He struck surely at the ghost within my guard. Unable to defend, he was cut through by successive strikes from Beatstick's blade. He vanished quickly. "Regroup," I shouted as Giantslayer's scales were sliced again. His blood splashed over the soldiers like a wave against rocks!

I spun, letting my rapiers reach the ghost behind me. Freya carved through his armour. I slipped away before he could react.

With my back against Beatstick's, I observed. Our force of magic threw more spells behind me. Giantslayer rushed into view. His body was nearly broken. Sweat poured down his face and mixed with his blood. Red footprints formed puddles behind him. Taking a deep breath, he grabbed a potion from his satchel and doused his wary body with its magical aid. Pouring it atop his head and finishing it with a swift gulp, he tightened his lance. He was ready for our final charge.

Caelynn's focused expression was replaced with fear. I turned toward Gwenovyn. I couldn't see her magical barrier anymore. She readied a response to Caelynn's attacks. A large sphere of flames grew between her hands as her sinister smile dissolved within a passionate raging stare. Our entire party was gathered within the proximity of an explosive spell. She corralled us! Gwenovyn reached her hands overhead as the flames expanded. Relishing in the thought of turning us into crisped corpses, she held her spell as it grew.

"Caelynn!" I shouted.

"Way ahead of you!" Our mage's fireball collided with Gwenovyn's. *'BFOOM!'* They exploded within her grasp!

After shielding my eyes, I saw that her concentration was broken. The elven ghosts were gone. Two of her shields were missing as well; both at her right side where smoke rose from the stones around her. The opening we needed was revealed. Beatstick ran beside Gwenovyn. He swung at her ghostly form with no dwarven defense to contest him. Ardronel charged behind him. His corporeal fists landing hard against her body.

"ENOUGH!" she shouted. A wave of turquoise magic resonated from within her. The remaining ghosts disappeared as her spirit floated higher. Her body emitted the same ghostly flames that adorned the walls. Her face hid none of her rage. "You've interfered long enough! This is my place of rest! It's my revenge! You have no right to disrupt my afterlife! This is my sacred tomb full of everything that ever mattered. My last connection to this... My... My beloved!" Tears dripped from her eyes.

I felt a deep pain pierce my heart. While I've rushed to the aid of many damsels in distress throughout my travels, never had I seen a woman so distressed in this way. Every blade that sliced my flesh here, every deadly blow that I parried; they were but pieces of her anguish. All of it, even before we arrived, each strike from every battle were but reactions to her soul crushing despair. The small fraction of her sorrow that I could feel through mere empathy was enough to overwhelm me. Our force of benevolence would act again.

I stepped slowly towards her and caught her eye. Feeling a tear roll down my cheek, I watched her ferocious expression drift towards confusion. "Hell hath no fury like a woman scorned... and who has been more scorned than you?" I presented my majestic swords as I moved closer. I said each name aloud before returning them to their sheaths. "Jezebel... Freya... so aptly named for their ability to pierce the heart in the same pinpointed and devastating ways that only a lover can." I took a knee and gazed upon her. "You, Gwenovyn, were so struck in life that your pain pierced beyond your heart and into your very soul, binding it to this place. How long were the two of you in love?"

Her spirit calmed and sank slightly toward the ground. "Three hundred and forty years."

"And how many *thousands* of years have you spent recreating the same bloodshed?"

"Four thousand, three hundred, and forty-six."

I nodded slowly. "Don't you think-"

"Maybe it's time to move on," Caelynn rolled her eyes.

I cleared my throat, "Well yes, but perhaps not letting *one* experience outweigh the oth-"

"We found the journal of the woman that seduced your husband," Beatstick rushed. Gwenovyn's eyes lit aflame as she turned to him. "The handmaiden was a spy. She was sent by the humans and dwarves to infiltrate the sylvan domain by way of your *husband* and trick him by leading him here to his death."

"I KNOW THIS ALREADY," she shouted, "Why do you think I've done all this?" The flames that engulfed her brightened. Still, on one knee, I reacted with nimble fingers. I pulled parchment and charcoal from my satchel. With the same lethal speed which I wield my espadas roperas, I sketched her. Gwenovyn rose higher as she shrieked, ready to send us all beyond. "She took EVERYTHING from me!" My party braced. I finished!

"Gwenovyn!" I reached my arms in front of me. Hands on top and bottom, I displayed the image of her hate-filled, ghostly expression. My voice lowered, I asked her plainly, "Do you even recognize yourself anymore?" The room fell silent. My party's glances darted at each other.

Her fires dimmed. She paused as she stared at the parchment before her. The honest depiction moved her in the way only true artistry can. Its power of romanticism overwhelmed her. An orange hue engulfed the once turquoise room as the surrounding torches returned to their original glow. "I," she said before descending to the ground, "...I see now." Like a blanketed flame, she was gone.

The Elemental

GWENOVYN

Epilogue

So was the climax to a tale spanning two ages. The tragic consequences of deceit, greed, and heartbreak were woven like a noose around poor Gwenovyn's neck. Her torment finally ended; a great weight is lifted from the shoulders of this world. I pray that in the great beyond she finds a time of peace equal in grandeur to her past suffering. Perhaps a reunion with her beloved, at the very least.

Ardronel is gone. Within moments of Gwenovyn's passing, he vanished amid a peaceful expression of gratitude. There was a sombre moment of silence that followed...

As I scribble my final words of this harrowing tale, I reflect. During this dive into the pits of the earth, I was but a humble witness to many great sites. A historic battle, a terrible curse, a wretched contortion of love. I saw Caelynn's resourcefulness when cornered and the peak of Giantslayer's overwhelming thrusts. I found a new ally, perhaps, in the cunning mercenary Beatstick. I laid a new friend, Ardronel, to rest. *Could I have also learned something along the way?*

Why yes, I have! As I continue to journey from deed to greater deed, it remains true that; through every breach through the unknown, march up a guarded tower, or even decent into flaming depths, the truest pleasures come from the small victories one watches their companions make along the way. Here at the base of this newly recovered realm, I learned the victory cherished the most can sometimes be that of a once greatest foe.

So, I recorded my allies and me together in this room. I made use of the bountiful lighting and rearranged the torches to aid in the creation of a final piece of art. A canvas painting depicting not only Giantslayer, Caelynn, Beatstick, and I, but the body of our new friend Gwenovyn as well. Her once scorned soul put finally to rest by becoming beloved once again.

It appears Giantslayer's finished collecting samples of the elemental's corpse. Caelynn and Beatstick seem to be ending their discussion on reactive combat. ...All seems concluded. Yes, I hear my companions call out to me that they're ready to depart. Now begins the journey up the spiralling city *...and to what next exactly?*

Only time will tell where the four forces, leaving behind this now cleansed piece of the past, are headed. One thing, though, is certain. Our work *here* is done.

Signed,

Maximilian
Napoleon
Luciano
Donnadieu!

www.ingramcontent.com/pod-product-compliance
Lightning Source LLC
Chambersburg PA
CBHW071008120726
47910CB00004B/1438